123

D1309067

On *Sesame Street,*
Gordon is played by Roscoe Orman.

Library of Congress Cataloging-in-Publication Data:
Hautzig, Deborah. Get well, Granny Bird. (A Sesame Street start-to-read book) Featuring Jim Henson's Sesame Street Muppets. SUMMARY: Though Big Bird makes a mess trying to help Granny get well, she appreciates the fact that he came. ISBN: 0-394-82247-1 (trade); 0-394-92247-6 (lib. bdg.) [1. Sick — Fiction. 2. Grandmothers — Fiction. 3. Puppets — Fiction] I. Mathieu, Joseph, ill. II. Children's Television Workshop. III. Title. IV. Series: Sesame Street start-to-read books. PZ7.H2888Ge 1989 [E] 88-18446

Manufactured in the United States of America   1 2 3 4 5 6 7 8 9 0

A Sesame Street Start-to-Read Book™

Get Well, Granny Bird

by Deborah Hautzig
illustrated by Joe Mathieu

Featuring Jim Henson's Sesame Street Muppets

Random House/Children's Television Workshop

Big Bird was reading a letter
when Gordon came along.
"Big Bird, you look so sad!"
said Gordon. "What's the matter?"
"Granny Bird has a cold,"
Big Bird told him.
"And I am worried."

"Don't worry, Big Bird," said Gordon.
"A cold doesn't make you very sick.
  Granny just needs to rest
  and stay warm and drink a lot.
  Then she will be fine."
  Suddenly Big Bird
  had an idea.
"I will go to Granny's house,"
  he said.
  He got out his suitcase.
"I will take care of Granny,"
  he said.
"I will help her get well!"

Gordon took Big Bird to the bus.

They waved good-bye.

"Tell Granny to get well soon,"

called Gordon.

The bus took Big Bird
right to Granny's little house
on the beach.
"Yoo-hoo, Granny! Surprise!"
shouted Big Bird.

"Big Bird!" said Granny.

"What a nice surprise."

"I came to help you get well,"
   said Big Bird. "Now go back to bed
   and I will make some soup for you!"

He opened a can
of noodle soup.

PLOP!
He dumped
the soup
into a bowl.

"Here comes lunch!"
called Big Bird.

Granny tasted the soup and said,
"This is lovely, Big Bird.
But I think I will heat it up
a little."

Granny heated her soup
and made a nice birdseed sandwich
for Big Bird.
"Did you like the lunch I made?"
asked Big Bird.
"Oh, yes—ACHOO!" sneezed Granny.
"Go back to bed, Granny!" said Big Bird.

Granny got back into bed.
"Gordon says you have to stay warm,"
said Big Bird.
He opened his suitcase
and took out his woolly winter scarf
and his fuzzy earmuffs.

He wrapped the scarf
around Granny's neck
and put the earmuffs on her head.
"Are you warm now?" he asked.
"Yes, dear," said Granny.
"Very warm."

"Now I will read you
a story," said Big Bird.
He read very slowly.
It was a long story.
Granny yawned.
At last Big Bird said,
"The end."

"Now what can I do to help you
get well?" asked Big Bird.
"The doctor says I must gargle
with salt water," said Granny.
"Can you bring me some?"
Big Bird said, "Don't move!
I know where there is
lots of salty water!"

Big Bird got his bucket
and ran down to the beach.
"Wow! Look at all this
salty seawater!" he said.
He sat down in the wet sand
and filled his bucket with water.

Big Bird took the water to Granny.

"I see you went to the beach,"
said Granny.

"Gee, how can you tell?" he asked.

Granny smiled and said,

"There is sand on the floor, dear."

Granny got her broom
and swept up the sand.
Then she said,
"I will take a little nap now,
and you can play
on the porch, Big Bird."

Big Bird went to the porch.

"I will jump rope,"
he said to himself.

"Jumpety bumpety thumpety rope,
Granny's almost well, I hope,"
he sang out loud.

And the rope went
THUMP, THUMP, THUMP.

"Big Bird, dear," called Granny.

"Can you please be
a little more quiet?"

So Big Bird stopped jumping rope.
He sat on the porch swing.
"Swinging is very quiet,"
  he whispered to himself.
  But the swing went
  CREAK, CREAK, CREAK.
"Granny, are you still sleeping?"
  called Big Bird.
"Yes," she said in a sleepy voice.
"Do you want a glass of water?"
  asked Big Bird.
"No, dear. I just want to rest,"
  said Granny.

After a while
Big Bird got more and more lonely.
"I wonder if Granny needs me,"
he said. "I think I will go see
how she is feeling."

He tiptoed into Granny's room.
She was fast asleep.

"Granny," whispered Big Bird loudly.
"Are you still sleeping?"
  Granny opened her eyes.
"No, Big Bird, not anymore,"
  she said.
"Good! Now I can make supper
  for you," he said.

Big Bird looked on the kitchen shelf.

"I will make some yummy rice!"

he said.

He reached for the box of rice,

and then...CRASH!

He tripped on his jump rope.

Granny ran to the kitchen.
Big Bird was on the floor.
So was all the rice.
Big Bird began to cry.
"I can't do anything right,"
he sobbed. "The soup was cold.
I got sand on the floor.
I woke you up,
and now I made a mess!
And I just wanted to help!"

"But, Big Bird, you did help!"
said Granny. "Just seeing you
makes me feel better."
Big Bird stopped crying.
"Really?" he asked.
"Yes," said Granny.
"I think my cold is almost gone,
thanks to my sweet little Big Bird."
And she gave him a big hug.